Everyone's Child

MoBoni Lewis

Everyone's Child

MoBoni Lewis

Paperback Edition First Published in Great Britain
in 2016 by aSys Publishing

eBook Edition First Published in Great Britain
in 2016 by aSys Publishing

Disclaimer
This is a work of fiction. Names, characters, businesses,
places, events and incidents are either the products of
the author's imagination or used in a fictitious manner.
Any resemblance to actual persons, living or dead, or
actual events is purely coincidental.

ISBN: 978-1-910757-54-3
aSys Publishing 2016

This book is dedicated to everyone in need of a miracle.

Acknowledgements

To my nearest and dearest, a very big "Thank you" for your unwavering support and encouragement. You made those very long nights of writing and re-writing bearable. Thank you so much.

To my dear friend, Rosa, my "product tester" as I call her, your enthusiasm is infectious. Thank you for believing in me.

And to God, Almighty, the giver of life, Thank you for the gift of writing. I couldn't have done this without you; I owe it all to you!

Chapter One

It was Agnes's last night in Lose. The whole village had gathered to say their "farewells", with little parcels of food in tow—Agnes was everyone's child.

The first to gain admission into a higher education institution in her community, Agnes Kembe soon became a "celebrity," as news of the young orphan girl who had made it into the prestigious Semple college hit the headlines.

And with her parents long gone, the whole village had chipped in to ensure that the young Agnes was able to pursue her dreams of becoming a school teacher.

"You've made us all proud," Kiki Gimera whispers into Agnes's ear, as the young girl passed round loose packets of Corn biscuit and fried bean cakes, all of which were instantly swiped off the plate, as eager little hands reached out in quick succession. Agnes smiles, shyly, she wasn't expecting to go this far, but the villagers had always been there for her, especially her aunt, Kiki, on whose account the college fees had been settled.

* * *

Half an hour later, and it was time for Agnes to leave, and almost immediately Kiki began to sob, and was soon joined by friends, Teni and Bawa, crying and bawling their eyes out, each desperately trying to outdo the other. And then everyone else began to cry, including the kids who had been happily munching away a few minutes earlier, their oily lips, glistening in the dark.

Agnes was perplexed—she was only going to school. Ten minutes later, however, having been able to convince her family and friends that she could always come home, especially at Christmas time, the young Agnes was soon on her way to Semple, little realizing that her life was about to change, forever.

* * *

Agnes Kembe (Kembe, being her mother's maiden name) had lived with the Gimeras for the last seventeen years of her life, clueless as to how she had become an Orphan—it was a well-kept secret, known only to a few within the community. And with so many versions of the events surrounding her birth, the exact details of which have also been kept a secret, the young Agnes soon gave up trying to find her roots.

As a young girl, however, Agnes had often wondered what her mother Tana, looked like, there were no photographs of her anywhere, not even with her mother's sister, Kiki. And her father, no one really talked about him, except, of course, to say that he was dead. But deep down, Agnes knew the Gimeras had a lot to answer for, especially Kiki, whose nose would often twitch at the mention of her sister's name and whose stories never seemed to add up, no matter how cleverly woven they were.

But this was Lose, keeping secrets was a part of everyday life, the one thing that kept them together and perhaps the only thing that could one day, pull them apart. And until then, Agnes Kembe knew she was going to have to accept herself for who she was, and with it, was a strong determination to succeed.

Chapter Two

Known for its reputation for attracting the best of students, Semple college was in a class of its own. And so, when Agnes Kembe showed up in a yellow dress and matching head scarf, after an eight-hour bus ride, that had left her looking worse for wear, many were stunned, not to say the least.

"Can I help you?" the security guard asks, on sighting Agnes, looking her over suspiciously as she approached the gates.

"I'm Agnes Kembe, a new student," Agnes stutters, her eyes welling up—she could tell almost immediately, that she wasn't welcomed.

"Of course, the Orphan girl," the guard returns. "This way then," he motions, with his fingers, revealing a pair of very expensive-looking rings.

Agnes followed her head held high—she'd earned the right to be at Semple, and no one was going to take that away from her.

* * *

But life at Semple soon became a dread for the young Agnes. The more she'd tried to fit in, the more she'd been ignored. It was almost as if she was invisible, as the other students dashed in and out of classes, completely oblivious to her desire for friendship.

And so one afternoon, after several days of being left on her own, she decided to approach one of the girls she'd seen around a few times—a strikingly beautiful young girl, called Pamela Lake.

"I like your hair," Agnes tells her, almost in awe.

"Thanks," Pamela replies, doing a flick. "They are Fusion Extensions."

"Fusion extensions?"

"Yeah!"

"You've never heard of that?"

"Not really!"

Pamela nearly passed out in shock. "You've got a lot to learn, girl," she whispers into Agnes's ear, strutting off.

Agnes felt slighted—her hair had been neatly cornrowed. It was what everyone in Lose had. From then on, Agnes Kembe made up her mind to get Fusion extensions, like Pamela Lake, the only problem was, how?

* * *

Two months on, and with hardly anyone to call a "friend", Agnes began thinking of leaving Semple for good. She'd already missed a number of extra lectures, because as always no one was telling her anything.

And then she had a dream. The entire village community turned up at the school gate, asking her not to give up. She was all they had. Agnes knew in that moment that she had to complete her education, if not for herself, but for the many who had invested in her. She had to finish at Semple.

* * *

The following day, with renewed determination and an even stronger sense of purpose, Agnes Kembe attended every one of her lectures with an extra spring in her step. She was determined to make the most of what she had. But one thing still bothered Agnes, and very much too. Her short-sightedness had become the butt of regular jokes in and outside of class often reducing her to tears.

* * *

"Get your eyes fixed," Batty, one classmate taunts, as Agnes struggled to read the sitting arrangements from the back of the class. The whole class erupted into laughter amidst shouts of Batty! Batty!

Agnes Kembe began to sob, she'd always felt that her eyes needed attention, but with Kiki Gimera having consistently maintained that her niece's short-sightedness was due to an excessive consumption of crayfish, and nothing else, the young Agnes had learnt to live, without.

"And she's only got one outfit," another classmate hollers from across the room, referring, of course, to Agnes's yellow dress. Agnes ran out of the class, sobbing, this was more than she could take.

And that very week, armed with the little amount of money contributed by the villagers for her upkeep, Agnes Kembe hit the shops, buying as many outfits as she could, returning to school, almost penniless, but optimistic of making a few friends.

Chapter Three

"I almost didn't recognize you," Pamela squeals, admiring Agnes from every angle as they stood in line at the School Cafeteria.

Agnes smiles, preening herself, her skirt was now a few inches shorter, and her hair had been fixed, although not like Pamela's.

"How about joining the College Babes?" Pamela asks, quietly. "A few of the girls are finishing this year and we could do with a new face on the block."

Agnes Kembe could hardly contain her joy. "Of course!" She replies, almost choking.

"Get dressed and be ready for six, then," Pamela returns, casually, "and take care of yourself, we have a party this evening."

Agnes ran to the hostel almost immediately, and a few hours later, dressed in one of her newest outfits; the young Agnes was ready to party.

* * *

Not one to play around with words, Pamela Lake was at Agnes's at six on the dot, with her group, dressed to the nines.

"Oh my!" She shrieks on seeing Agnes's outfit.

Agnes Kembe began heading for the door in haste, only to be pulled back by one of the other girls-her name was Doris Bay.

"Don't embarrass the poor girl," Doris tells Pamela, giving Agnes a big hug.

"Alright, she does, look nice," Pamela concedes, grudgingly, looking Agnes over, briefly, "but we don't do nice. We stand out!"

Agnes looked at the girls. They did stand out, alright, especially, Doris.

Suddenly, Pamela let out a loud scream, her left hand firmly placed over her left eye.

"Are you alright?" Doris asks, anxiously, as the other girls began looking around for any signs of danger.

"It's gone," Pamela blurts out, her left hand still over her left eye.

"What has?" the girls ask in unison.

"My false eyelashes," Pamela replies, tearfully.

Agnes Kembe stifles a laugh as the girls began searching high and low for Pamela's "prop".

"Here it is," Doris calls out, a few minutes later, planting the lashes back on Pamela's heavily made-up eyes. And with the "prop" back in place, the girls crammed themselves into a waiting taxi for the ten-minute drive to town.

Chapter Four

The party was already in full swing when the girls arrived. Young men in suspenders and bowler hats paraded the room, eager to please the ladies, and, of course, everyone knew one another.

Agnes stood in a corner, expecting to be ushered in like the other girls, but no one pays her any attention.

"You're going to be alright," the young Agnes tells herself, and with steely determination headed straight for the gallery.

* * *

On the other side of the hall, Pamela Lake and her on-off boyfriend, Lance Tega were making up after yet another falling out.

"And who's that girl?" Lance quizzes on spotting Agnes Kembe at the gallery.

"My new friend," Pamela replies, playing with his bowler hat. "I invited her."

"She's been by herself all evening," Lance points out, looking intently in Agnes's direction.

"And what's that got to do with you?" Pamela queries.

"Everything," Lance replies, standing to his feet. "It's my party."

* * *

With that, Lance Tega began making his way towards Agnes Kembe, and was soon introducing himself to her, as Pamela watched from afar.

Agnes put up a front, almost immediately. Aunt Kiki had already warned her about men with shifty eyes.

Not one to give up on a pretty face, however, Lance decides on a different approach. "Why don't you tell me about yourself, gorgeous," he purrs, pulling his chair up close to Agnes Kembe. Agnes's face breaks into a broad smile. No one had ever called her gorgeous, at least not in Semple.

Unaware of who Lance was, Agnes flirted with him all night long, laughing at his every joke. Lance was a perfect gentleman as far as she could see.

The other girls gave Agnes curious looks, as they passed by, but none said a word, as she drunk herself into a stupor.

By now, Pamela had, had enough, and in a fit of rage stormed out of the party, leaving Agnes to find her way back to the hostel.

Chapter Five

It's Sunday morning. Agnes Kembe stumbles out of bed, feeling light-headed and disorientated. The air was stale and reeked of alcohol and her room mates were nowhere in sight. Still groggy from the night before, she takes a few unsteady steps but was soon back on the bed, falling asleep almost immediately.

Two hours later and now with a much clearer head, Agnes began taking in her surroundings, but one thing was now clear. She wasn't in her room, but where was she? With hardly any recollection of the night before apart from having been at a party, and being chatted up, Agnes began looking around the room for clues, when suddenly the front door swung open and in walked Lance Tega, with a mug of coffee. Agnes's face lit up in an instant.

"So you brought me here," She exclaims with delight, jumping off the bed.

"It was the least I could do," Lance replies, casually, sipping on his coffee. "You were dead drunk and I didn't want to leave you behind."

Agnes pursed her lips in silence. She really did have too much to drink, but it was all an attempt to fit in, to show that she was no novice. "Thanks," she says, quietly, somewhat embarrassed at having made a fool of herself.

"So when do I see you next?" She asks Lance, shyly.

"There won't be a next time," comes the quiet, but firm response.

"But I thought you liked me," Agnes stutters, fighting back the tears.

"Yeah, I did, yesterday," Lance replies, as a matter of fact.

Agnes opens her mouth to speak, but no words come out.

"And don't hang around for too long," Lance tells her, as he heads for the door. "My parents will be coming to visit."

Agnes Kembe broke down in tears, almost immediately, she didn't need anyone to tell her that she'd fallen for the oldest trick in the book. Lance Tega wasn't the perfect gentleman she had thought he was.

* * *

Staggering out of Lance's, shoes in hand, Agnes tried all she could, to remember the last twelve hours of her life, but everything seemed blurry and her head ached and at this point, she became very emotional yet again, sobbing hysterically as she walked along, she had promised to stay true to herself but her desire for love and acceptance had taken over, so quickly, weakening her resolve.

Just then, a church bell began tolling in the distance-it was a call to worship. Although not particularly religious, the young Agnes felt a need to attend-she wanted to unburden her soul.

With that, Agnes Kembe began hurrying towards the building, shoes in hand, only to be stopped at the entrance. And having been unable to convince the Usher that she had indeed come in peace, her alcohol-laden breath suggesting otherwise, she was promptly marched off the premises, lest she disrupt the service as some have done.

Half an hour later, tired and scorched, Agnes waddled into school where an irate Pamela was on hand to receive her.

* * *

"He's mine!" Pamela shrieks as Agnes walked into the room. "Why did you spend the night with him?"

"I didn't ask to be taken over to his," Agnes replies, curtly, plonking herself on the bed.

That got her a slap from Pamela, almost immediately.

"Our friendship is over," Pamela tells her, screaming, "and I hope you remembered to take care of yourself because he doesn't do babies. I've been there before, many times."

Agnes holds her burning cheek and began to sob. By this time, however, a few other girls had joined in, having heard Pamela's screams from afar.

"We don't take what belongs to other people around here, village girl," one of the girls points out, rudely, pulling Agnes by the hair; her name was Sally Keys.

"I always knew she couldn't be trusted," another affirms, pushing Agnes against the wall.

Agnes Kembe fell on the floor, crying. Her troubles, it seemed, had only just begun.

Chapter Six

In Lose, however, the atmosphere was one of excitement as the people celebrated the arrival of the new yam. The harvest had been plenteous, and many had built new barns to store the surplus produce. The children played and sang about yam. It'd been a feast of yam all week-boiled yam, fried yam, roasted yam and er . . . yam.

A couple of young men, however, decided to use the opportunity to register their interest in Agnes Kembe, but Kiki Gimera wasn't taken any "Orders".

Agnes was now in a league of her own, she tells them, proudly, and only the handsomely rich need apply.

"You can keep her," one of the men, taunts, grabbing the basket of yams with which he had hoped to entice his prospective in-laws, and walking away, but Kiki hardly batted an eye lid. She was on a mission to find a husband for her niece, and only the best, yeah, the rich would do.

Chapter Seven

Agnes Kembe! The voice reverberated across the room. Agnes opened one eye, and then the other. And there, standing beside her desk was Ben Riddle, the Mathematics lecturer, looking very displeased or rather disappointed. Agnes was one of his favourite pupils.

"See me after class," Ben tells Agnes, angrily, walking back to the front of the class in haste.

* * *

Half an hour later and Agnes was at Ben Riddle's office.

"My lecture today must have been very boring!" Ben began, looking intently at Agnes Kembe.

"Not that, Sir," Agnes replies. "I was just very tired."

"Been staying up all night?"

"Not really."

"Why then were you sleeping in class?"

"I haven't eaten in days."

"You haven't?"

"No sir."

"And why's that?"

"I haven't got any money left."

Ben reaches for his wallet, almost immediately. He knows a little about Agnes's background. "Here, take this," he says, giving Agnes Kembe some money. "It's all I can offer you." Agnes's eyes widened.

"Thank you sir," she says excitedly, putting the money in her coat pocket.

"It's not a lot," Ben points out, "so you'll have to write home as soon as possible. I'm sure your aunt will be more than happy to send you some money. You've been a very good student."

Agnes nods, hurriedly, grateful to have gotten off lightly, but of course, writing home was out of the question; Kiki Gimera had already sold two fattened nanny goats that year, selling another to raise money was very unlikely.

* * *

And so, Agnes Kembe began washing dishes at the school cafeteria in exchange for food.

One evening, however, after a series of shifts, washing dishes in-between classes, she began feeling unwell and now two weeks late, this could only mean one thing- she was pregnant, or maybe not; she'd never been regular.

* * *

A quick trip to the Chemist, the following day, soon confirms Agnes's fears. She was indeed pregnant, and at this point, she began to panic. The college had strict rules about being pregnant outside of wedlock and she could end up being thrown out.

Everyone's Child

* * *

That same evening, Agnes Kembe decided to pay Lance Tega a visit. He was the only one she'd been with, since coming to Semple, but Lance was in total denial. It could have been anyone, he tells Agnes, bluntly, taking advantage of the fact that the young girl had been under the influence of alcohol at his party. Agnes threw herself at Lance and began to sob; all she'd ever wanted was to be a school teacher and now that opportunity was slipping away.

"Please, cover me; take my shame away," she pleads clawing at the floor with her bare hands until they bled, but Lance simply pushes her away.

* * *

Over the next few days, Agnes Kembe tried to talk Lance Tega into committing himself to a "relationship" with her, at least until the child was born. The stigma of having a child outside of wedlock in Lose often saw many girls being disowned by their families.

But Lance wasn't prepared to play happy families and simply threatens to reveal Agnes's "secret" to the school authorities if he wasn't left alone.

From then on, Agnes Kembe began looking for ways to hide her growing tummy until her clothes could no longer fit. And now faced with the prospect of being thrown out of school, with no qualifications and incurring the wrath of an entire village, many of whom had invested in her education, decides to terminate the pregnancy.

Chapter Eight

The Clinic in Kita was one of many "offices" in an old building, for which Agnes Kembe was grateful. Fifteen minutes later, however, and she was still unsure of where to go.

"Can I help you?" a very smiley young woman asks, on passing Agnes for the third time in ten minutes.

"No! I mean, yes!" Agnes replies, feeling somewhat embarrassed -she'd hoped to get everything "sorted", without having to talk to anyone else about her situation, but the doctor.

The woman looks directly at Agnes's slightly bulging tummy. "Is it an Evacuation you've come for?" She asks, casually.

"Evacu what?"

"E-V-A-C-U-A-T-I-O-N."

Agnes frowns, that didn't sound right. "I'm pregnant," she says, quietly, almost whispering.

"And you don't want to keep the baby?"

"No."

"Come with me, then," the woman tells her.

And with that, Agnes Kembe was escorted to a side room, where a few others were waiting to be attended to.

Everyone's Child

* * *

The room was very nicely decorated, and on the wall was a picture of a pretty young girl claiming to have gotten her life back. Agnes felt a sense of relief. Soon it will all be over, she tells herself. And then it was time for the procedure and almost immediately, Agnes began to sob, wringing her hands like a small child.

"You'll be alright," the nurse assures her, but Agnes shakes her head vigorously-these weren't the tears of a frightened 17-year-old, but of one who'd fallen for a lie.

Five hours later, very sore, but somewhat relieved at not having to put her dream on hold, Agnes Kembe was on her way back to School, but deep within her was a void, a sense of guilt, knowing she'd denied another the right to life in order to pursue hers.

Chapter Nine

But any promise of moving on soon eluded the young Agnes. Her heart ached for several weeks after the termination and all she saw in her dreams were babies, one of whom seemed to make a regular appearance.

One morning, after yet another night of wild dreams, Agnes Kembe could take it no more. Going before the Lord, she asks to be forgiven, for taking the life of an innocent child, and for the first time in weeks, was able to sleep through the night, waking up to the sound of singing—her own, and her eyesight had miraculously improved. Agnes knew in that moment that she had indeed been forgiven.

* * *

Intrigued by this God who could clean a person inside-out, the young Agnes began meeting up with a group of students after school to learn more about the Lord and was soon telling others, including Pamela Lake about the love that had set her free. But Pamela was unyielding. One termination was bad enough, she tells herself, but four, were unforgiveable; four innocent lives snuffed out in order to keep her boyfriend. Surely, the Lord must hate someone like her.

However, Pamela soon learnt to forgive herself, while yielding her soul to the Lord, and together with Agnes began spreading the love of God to other young girls who had found themselves in similar situations.

Three years later, Agnes Kembe graduated from Semple College, with distinction and so did Pamela Lake, but not Lance Tega, who a year earlier had been thrown out for his wild ways.

Chapter Ten

Soon after returning to Lose, Agnes Kembe became inundated with several marriage proposals. But with none of the would-be-grooms able to afford her bride price, as set by Kiki and her husband, Lajo, the men soon returned to their various homes, hugely disappointed.

And then one afternoon, a young man walked into the village, asking for Agnes by name. He was Kamil Benson, a former college mate of Agnes. Now a successful business man, all Kamil needed was a wife, and he could think of no other, but Agnes Kembe.

Agnes was very surprised at Kamil's visit- she'd only told him where she lived in passing and didn't think he'd taken note. But the two were soon reminiscing about their college days and then of course, Kamil explains the purpose of his visit.

Agnes was overjoyed- Kamil was also a Christian and was one of those who'd encouraged her on her journey of faith, and she liked him too. In typical Lose style, however, the young man was asked to return the following month with his people, but only if he could afford Agnes's bride price.

* * *

Exactly four weeks later, Kamil Benson was back in Lose, with his parents, and was soon allowed to see Agnes in private, while the prospective in-laws wined and dined in situ.

"There's something you need to know," Agnes blurts out to Kamil, as soon they were alone, not wanting to start the relationship on deception.

"Okay! What is it?"

"Erm . . ."

"Erm, what?"

"I'm not proud of it, but I thought you should know."

"Know what?"

"I 've been touched. I'm not a virgin."

Kamil holds his head in shock. "So why tell me now?" He quizzes, his lips quivering.

"I needed to be sure that you'll be back," Agnes replies, quietly.

Kamil began pacing the room, suddenly realizing the enormity of the decision he was about to make; he loved Agnes, no doubt, but perhaps it was better to withdraw the marriage proposal now, he tells himself, than allow Agnes Kembe to be humiliated on her big day.

* * *

By now Agnes was in tears-she'd taken a chance on Kamil, in the hope that the young man would see beyond her "fault", but that decision seemed to have gone against her.

"I can understand," she tells Kamil, amidst tears, "and I don't hold it against you."

But Kamil was silent.

* * *

In the living room, however, Kamil's parents were becoming very uncomfortable. They were yet to see Agnes Kembe, but the Gimeras were already on the third bottle of wine.

"So when can we see our bride?" Kamil's mother, Hana, asks, eager to get the ball rolling, at least before the Gimeras got their hands on the fourth and last bottle of wine.

"I'll get her for you," Kiki offers, tipsily, but was soon on the floor, rolling her head and laughing loudly.

Lajo stands up, quickly in an attempt to save his wife from further embarrassment, but being ten stones lighter, ends up in a heap right beside her, in the most undignified manner.

The Bensons stare at their prospective in-laws in disbelief, and without warning Kamil's Father, Fala grabs the last bottle of wine, keeping it out of sight.

* * *

With her dreams of becoming a bride slowly ebbing away, Agnes Kembe began thinking of leaving Lose for good. It was only a matter of days before the whole village knew she'd been "touched". She'd rather be a single woman in the city, she tells herself, than be shamed by the very people who had once sung her praise.

And then suddenly, Kamil was on one knee. "Marry me, Agnes," he says, quietly. Agnes blinked several times, just to make sure she was seeing right. "Are you really sure you want to do this?" She asks, her lips quivering. Kamil nods, gently.

Agnes cups her face in her hands and began to weep-she was going to be a bride at last.

* * *

Soon afterwards, Agnes was telling Kamil about Lance, how the young man had taken advantage of her, and how she had terminated the pregnancy in order to stay in school.

"I don't judge you, Agnes," Kamil says, quietly.

"Thank you," Agnes replies, even more quietly.

"But you still haven't accepted my proposal," Kamil reminds her holding out his hand.

"Yes!" Agnes blurts out, taking Kamil's hands in hers.

"I'll stand by you, Agnes," Kamil affirms, "and Thank you, for being truthful."

The marriage proposal was concluded later that evening, with the Bensons handing over Agnes's bride price to the Gimeras in full view of the villagers.

* * *

Six months later, Kamil and Agnes tied the knot in a simple but classy ceremony. Kiki Gimera, of course, was more than happy to give her niece away now that the family's demands had been met- Kamil had been very generous in his offer, with a portion of Agnes's bride price going to all those who had helped raise her.

The village photographer stood at attention, capturing every pose. This was, indeed, a day to remember.

* * *

And then it was time for Kamil to leave with his bride, and at that point, Agnes began to sob. The Gimeras were the only family she'd known, plus it was considered inappropriate for a bride to be dry-eyed or overly excited on her wedding day. And so, Agnes gave it her all, sobbing profusely, as the drummers sung her praise. It was her final farewell to Lose until she came visiting as Agnes Benson.

Half an hour later, accompanied by Esther Saba, her maid of honour, Agnes Kembe was escorted out of her childhood home into the Benson family bus; She (Agnes) was now a Benson wife.

* * *

Kiki and Lajo watched in silence as the mini bus pulled out of the compound, their eyes, laden with tears. Agnes had made them proud, and of course, wealthier. Dalu, the Gardener, and Reya, the Cook snuck out of their rooms for a few minutes to catch a glimpse of Agnes as the bus sped past the servants' quarters, wondering if they'd ever see her again. And even though the people of Lose were sad to see Agnes leave their midst, her success had paved a way for other young girls in the village, many of who now saw her as a role model.

* * *

Arriving at Kamil's however, the young couple was soon besieged by a cheering crowd. At one end of the room was Caroline Bure, Kamil's former girl-friend, looking as gorgeous as ever, her long hair swept to one side.

Agnes's heart skipped a beat. Caroline had never really given up on Kamil, often telling the young man that she was his "first love", and bound to return. I'm Kamil's bride, Agnes tells herself, blissfully, as Caroline sashayed up and down doing her very best to get noticed, but no one pays her any attention.

* * *

Everyone's Child

Suddenly, one of the older wives raised a welcome song—it was time to usher the new bride into the family. Agnes began to sob, quietly -perhaps she ought not to have bothered getting married, she tells herself as the women began ushering her into the family house, the same ones that would demand to know her "status" by morning.

* * *

In another part of the house, Kamil Benson was being briefed by Papa Gobi, the clan head. Kamil was to openly declare his bride's "status" in the morning, to prove that the Bensons hadn't been short-changed, an offence that could see the Gimeras having to refund Agnes's bride price, together with an undisclosed amount of money to be agreed by both families.

It was one of the few times that Papa Gobi got to exercise his authority, unchallenged, and he was determined to show that he was in charge. "So you know what you have to do," He tells Kamil, licking his teeth as he plays with a half-eaten piece of kola. Kamil nods, seething. Of course he knew. No fewer than five men had gotten married in the last ten months alone.

* * *

The next morning, as early as 6.00am, a large crowd began gathering in front of the Benson family house- it was time to hear the "verdict" on the new bride. A couple of young girls had even dressed up as "replacements brides" in case Agnes was found to be wanting, as Kamil would then be expected to pick a new bride from those present. And of course, Caroline was on hand to grace the occasion, looking as gorgeous as ever.

Papa Gobi sat on his famous chair, his tiny feet hardly touching the ground as he prepares to announce whether the newest addition to the Benson wives had been "touched" or not, as was the custom. Kamil's mother Hana sat a few metres away, hands clasped over her head in anxious expectation, watching every move of the clock.

By 7.00am, there was hardly any place to stand, let alone sit. It was one of the largest crowds of its kind in the tiny village of Lekemu. The villagers spoke in low tones, their eyes glued to the door of the Benson family house as they waited for Kamil to appear with the "evidence".

But it soon became evident that they'd been outsmart-ed-Kamil had spent the night outside the village-he wasn't going to allow his wife to be put on trial again. Agnes had made mistakes, no doubt, but the Lord had forgiven her. He wasn't going to allow her to be judged all over again.

Papa Gobi ranted inaudibly for several seconds, displeasure boldly written across his wrinkled face-no one had ever called his bluff. The villagers, of course, knew that the show was over and began taking their leave, with many heading straight for the farm. The elders felt insulted and vowed to find Kamil, but with many of them having benefited from the young man's generosity, the matter was soon swept under the raffia mat.

Chapter Eleven

The Bensons began thinking of starting a family almost immediately. Kamil was an only child and was very keen to have a brood of his own. Some eight months later, however, while Kamil was away on business, Agnes began having severe stomach cramps, and for the first two days, dosed heavily on pain killers.

But she was soon at the hospital, only to be told that her womb was heavily infected- the only option was surgery.

Agnes held her tummy in agony and wept—she was only twenty- two. "Have you had a termination by any chance?" the doctor asks, looking intently at Agnes Benson.

Agnes nods, gently.

"How long ago was this?"

"A few years back."

"Well, it's the root cause of the infection from what I can see, the doctor affirms, holding out Agnes's x-ray. "Your womb was scarred in the process and is now heavily infected. We'll have to operate, immediately, if you're going to be around for much longer."

"Can I have some time to myself please?" Agnes asks, tearfully. "I need to speak to my husband; he needs to know I'm here."

But Kamil couldn't be reached-he was in some remote village, sourcing out raw materials for a new line of business. Agnes tried to hold out for as long as she could in the hope that Kamil would call, but with the pain in her abdomen hardly easing, and her life, now even more at risk, and she was soon signing the consent form to have her womb taken out.

Five and half hours later, heavily sedated and womb-less, Agnes Benson was wheeled into a recovery room, only to wake up to the sound of crying babies in the adjacent room. Agnes began to cry. This was one thing she was never going to be able to do, she tells herself and then of course her mind went to Kamil-how was she going to tell him that she could no longer give him the children he so desperately wanted.

Chapter Twelve

Three days later, a very excited Kamil returns home, with a tiny football jersey under his arms. "For our son," He announces, dropping the little jersey onto Agnes's lap as he tries to hug her. Agnes flinches, pushing him away.

"Aren't you happy to see me?" Kamil queries, somewhat taken aback by his wife's very unwelcoming reaction.

"Of course, I am," Agnes replies, forcing a smile. "Let me get you something to eat," but she was soon on the floor, groaning in pain.

'What happened?" Kamil asks, worriedly.

Agnes suddenly burst into tears, telling her husband all that had taken place while he was away.

Kamil's eyes' widened. "You mean . . . ," He stammers, pointing in the direction of Agnes's tummy.

Agnes nods, crying.

Kamil holds his head in his hands and began to sob-he so desperately wants a child, and a son in particular, to carry on the family name, and of course, without a child of his own, everything he'd worked for could soon end up in the hands of his half-siblings, who all along had been trying to lay claim to all he owned.

* * *

For the next hour, Agnes and Kamil sobbed, each helping to comfort the other, followed by a period of quiet contemplation.

"At least we still have each other," Kamil concludes, amidst tears, putting the little jersey away.

Agnes felt horrendously guilty, sobbing all night long-she'd denied her husband the one thing he really, really wanted.

* * *

Over the next few days, Kamil Benson began thinking of getting justice for his wife. Perhaps Agnes would have been able to give him a child or two if she still had a womb, he thought to himself.

But the clinic where the termination was carried out had ceased to exist and all records "destroyed", he was told .

The Bensons felt cheated; they didn't have a case and with Kamil's parents often turning up unannounced, asking for a grandchild, Agnes and Kamil decided to relocate further north to a little town called Muna-it was all they could think of to maintain their sanity.

Chapter Thirteen

In the process of time, the Bensons began looking to adopt. They'd given hope of ever having children, and have stopped attending church or any Christian gathering, managing, however, to keep their faith alive simply by praying before bedtime as Agnes was prone to nightmares.

Several months later, while teaching in a primary school, Agnes soon became attached to a sweet little girl called Didi Temas.

"Are you alright, Miss?" Didi would often ask, whenever she saw Agnes looking sad, until one day, she(Didi) decided to invite Agnes to church-Didi's father was a preacher, who according to the young Didi, was the best preacher in the world.

Reluctantly, Agnes agreed to attend, but enjoyed the service so much that she and Kamil soon made it their home church, and their once static faith began to grow again, until Didi's father Liddo, announced his retirement.

Agnes was distraught-the Temas had been like a second family as Kamil was often away from home.

* * *

At about the same time, the Bensons learnt that their adoption had come through-a young unmarried mother was giving her son away. Agnes and Kamil could hardly contain their joy and the following day, armed with a few baby clothes and a gift for Amy Prince, the young mother, who, had decided to give them the most precious gift that anyone could give to another, made their way to Paye.

* * *

Amy had opted for a private adoption, so private that she would only agree to meet at a rented apartment-she was only 15 and still in school, and hadn't the slightest idea who the baby's father was.

Five hours later, exhausted but equally excited at the prospect of being parents, the Bensons pulled up outside the rented apartment in the remotest part of Paye. Kamil hugs his wife, in quiet anticipation-they were going to be parents at last, when suddenly Agnes spots a slouchy figure in the distance and he looked very familiar indeed. "Are you sure we are in the right place?" She asks Kamil, nervously.

"Of course! I've got it clearly written out here," Kamil replies, looking at the address yet again, and reading it out, loudly. Just then the man turned round and it was exactly as Agnes had suspected- it was Lance Tega.

Agnes began feeling faint and immediately held on to her husband for support. "Are you alright?" Kamil asks, seeing Agnes's pained expression. Agnes nods, giving a weak smile.

"I know how you feel. I'm just as nervous as you are," Kamil points out, squeezing Agnes's hands.

* * *

A few minutes later, Kamil was introducing himself to Lance. "I'm Kamil Benson and this is my wife, Agnes," he began, extending his hands towards a very pale Lance, who had equally recognized Agnes.

"Lance Tega, Amy's father," Lance replies, nervously, making his way quickly towards the apartment.

Agnes couldn't believe her ears. How come she was ending up with Lance's grand-child out of all the babies waiting to be adopted, she tells herself. Life, really was being cruel to her. And of course, Agnes was the last person that Lance was expecting to see -his daughter had simply told him she was giving her baby away to a Mrs. Benson, with whom she had been speaking over the phone. Little did he know that it was Agnes Kembe.

* * *

"The Bensons are here, Honey," Lance announces to his daughter, from outside, only to ask the young girl, a few moments later, if she was sure about giving the child away.

"Of course, Dad," Amy replies, now getting frustrated. "I thought that was what you wanted."

"Just having second thoughts," Lance replies, casually. "Maybe we should go," Agnes interjects quickly, hoping to use the opportunity as a quick getaway-the last thing she wanted was a constant reminder of Lance in her home.

Kamil gives his wife a questioning look-he hadn't seen that coming. "Can you give us a minute, please," He tells Lance, dragging Agnes outside for a quick chat. "What's going on?" He asks, looking his wife straight in the eye. "You haven't been yourself ever since we got here, and now you are asking to leave. Is there something I should know?"

"That's him," Agnes blurts out.

"Who?"

"Lance."

"The same Lance?"

"Yes!"

Kamil clenches his fist in anger and began pacing the floor. "Promise me you won't do anything irrational," Agnes pleads, seeing the very determined look on her husband's face.

"I promise," Kamil replies, through gritted teeth. But Kamil Benson couldn't see himself having Lance's grandson under his roof either and soon informs Amy that they'd decided not to adopt her baby.

The young girl broke down in tears, almost immediately, blaming her father for "messing" things up, but Lance could hardly reply-he was still too shocked at the way things had turned out.

* * *

But that night, Lance Tega was unable to sleep. Seeing Agnes wanting to adopt could only mean one thing-she hadn't been able to have children or maybe not, but he was determined to find out, and of course, he still owed her an apology.

* * *

And so, very early the next morning, Lance Tega was on the phone to the Bensons, but it was Kamil who picked his call.

"Hello, It's Lance, Amy's father. Can I speak to your wife, please?" He asks, his voice shaking.

Kamil was just about to lash out at him when he remembers the promise he'd made to Agnes the day before and soon cautions himself.

Just then Agnes walked into the room.

"It's Lance," Kamil tells her. "He wants to talk to you."

"What does he want?"

"I don't know, he asked for you."

"What can I do for you, Mr. Tega?" Agnes asks, coldly, on being passed the phone.

"I owe you an apology," Lance began, "and I know it's eighteen years late, but I hope you can still find it in your heart to forgive me. I tried to look for you, but no one knew where you were. They said you moved on."

Agnes grits her teeth in silence. Thereafter, Lance went on to tell Agnes how Amy had been drugged at a night club, ended up being pregnant only to show up at his door step after being thrown out by her step dad, Guy Prince, with whom his wife Daisy had run off, and who had adopted Amy as their child.

Agnes began to cry, quietly-what goes round does really come round, she thought to herself.

* * *

Kamil stood by watching his wife's every expression—he wasn't going to let Lance hurt her, ever again, but realizing, however, that this was one battle that Agnes would have to fight on her own, soon leaves the room.

"Agnes could you raise this baby for Amy, please?" Lance asks, almost pleading. "I know you'll make a good mother. I denied you the opportunity many years ago, and this is about the best way I can give something back to you. I know it's a hard decision and I can understand if you don't want to, but have a think about it. I'll be grateful if you do."

And with that Lance ends the call.

* * *

Agnes began sobbing uncontrollably-she was almost as guilty as Lance, if not more-she'd murdered her unborn child, but the Lord had forgiven her. How could she not forgive Lance?

With that, Agnes began asking the Lord for help in forgiving Lance Tega and so did Kamil-it was a real struggle for the Bensons, knowing they could never have children of their own.

But the Lord supernaturally imparted them with the grace to forgive Lance and to release him and four hours later, the Bensons finally let go.

Chapter Fourteen

I n Paye, however, a very frustrated Amy is making other plans to have her little boy adopted, having initially refused to hand him over to anyone else. But four days on and several long nights waking up to feed her newborn, and she was now ready to hand him over to anyone who would have him. And then the phone rang, and it was Agnes- she'd agreed together with Kamil to adopt the baby.

* * *

The following day, the Bensons were back in Paye. "I never thought I'd see you again," Lance exclaims as Agnes and Kamil walked into the apartment.

"Neither did we," Kamil replies, quietly, a little smile playing across his lips.

Amy could hardly contain her joy, either and began packing her baby's bag almost immediately.

'If you don't mind me asking, have you got children?" Lance asks, curiously. "We do, now, and thank you," Agnes replies, quietly.

* * *

An hour and a half later, and the Bensons were ready to leave, but not before Agnes had led Amy and Lance to the Lord. Amy cradles her son for the last time, a lone tear, falling freely down her left cheek.

"Thank you," she tells Agnes, quietly, as she hands the little boy over.

"Thank you," Agnes replies, giving the young girl a big hug.

Lance also reached out to Kamil in that moment, apologizing for the way he had treated Agnes while at school.

"All have been forgiven," Kamil tells him, with a smile.

* * *

With that, Agnes and Kamil began making their way back home, only to be introduced to their new life almost immediately, their little boy having reserved the "best" for the last.

Without as much as a word, Agnes reached for the diapers and lovingly changed her son, the first of many changes to come.

And a week later, at a gathering of a few close friends, the Bensons christened their little boy "Joy", for he'd brought immeasurable joy to their once very ordinary lives.

Kiki and Lajo weren't able to attend but sent their love. They'd never travelled out of Lose and found the journey to Muna, very daunting. However, Kamil's parents didn't attend, for "very personal" reasons.

* * *

Two and a half years later, the Bensons began looking to adopt, again, and this time, a baby girl. Joy was almost three and had begun asking for a little sister, with whom to share his toys. But the adoption rules were now much stricter, and the possibility of a private adoption, even slimmer than when they first started out.

Refusing to be discouraged, by the stricter and almost impossible new rules, however, Agnes and Kamil decided to register their interest with as many agencies as possible-they were determined to give their son a little brother or sister, against the odds.

Chapter Fifteen

"You think he'll be alright here?" Kamil asks Agnes for the up-tenth time, as they pulled into the parking lot of "Little Tots".

"I'm sure he will," Agnes affirms, confidently, adjusting Joy's back pack. "It's the best in town; I had it checked out, and Rae's daughter attends, too."

Kamil's face eases into a smile. He knows Rae King wouldn't settle for less. Rae was Agnes's best friend.

Some ten minutes later, Agnes and Kamil were waving off, their three-year-old son, who was off in a flash.

"I wonder why we worry," Kamil says, disappointedly, as Joy dashes off, without as much as a "Good-bye".

"But I told you he was going to be fine," Agnes points out, smiling.

* * *

Like every other parent, the Bensons were back at the nursery at Six o'clock, to pick up their son, but the little boy was nowhere to be found.

"Home time, Joy," Sally James, the Nursery proprietor calls out, repeatedly as other children began running out to meet their parents, but there was no response. Then the curtains parted, and Joy emerged from behind the blinds, his toy tractor clutched tightly to his chest; he'd been hiding.

"You'll be here again tomorrow," Sally assures him, gently prying the toy from his hands.

Joy wasn't impressed, and began heading towards the door, his head hung low, but the little boy soon spots his parents in the distance and began running towards them in excitement.

Kamil holds out his arms, expectantly, a huge smile across his face, as Joy lands in them, giggling loudly.

"And how was your first day?" Agnes asks, pulling his little boy's cheeks playfully.

"Made lots of friends," Joy replies, happily.

Chapter Sixteen

A few weeks later, Agnes received a letter from Kiki Gimera, asking to see her, urgently.

The Bensons felt a huge sense of guilt. They hadn't been in touch with the Gimeras for a while, and hoped they hadn't left it too late. Almost immediately, Kamil began making plans to travel down to Lose with his wife, but with no one to babysit Joy at such short notice, decides to stay at home.

Six and a half hours later, Agnes Benson was in Lose, and was soon being ushered into her childhood home by her cousin, Fay, Kiki's daughter.

* * *

Seated on the couch, like he'd always done, was Lajo Gimera, except that this time he wasn't smoking his pipe, and right beside him, looking very sullen, was his wife, Kiki.

Agnes rushed to greet her Uncle and Aunt. "I'm sorry I haven't been in touch all this while," she began, "I know I promised to ..."

"It's okay," Kiki replies, curtly.

Agnes retreats almost immediately. This wasn't the Aunt Kiki she knew, and Lajo wouldn't even look her in the face.

"Your parents asked to see you," Kiki says, quietly.

"What parents?" Agnes asks, confused. "I thought I was an orphan."

"Not exactly," Kiki replies, avoiding her niece's gaze.

"You mean my parents were alive all along?"

"I can explain," Kiki interjects, rising to her feet.

"Where are they? I want to see them," Agnes screams, her voice trailing into the night.

* * *

Just then, Dalu, the Gardener hobbles into the living room, followed closely by Reya, the Cook, looking frail. "We are your parents," Dalu says, quietly.

"No, you're not," Agnes replies, fiercely. "You are Papa Dalu, the Gardener and this is Mama Reya, the Cook."

"They are your parents," Lajo, affirms, his first words of the evening. "Dalu is indeed, your father. His real name is Roti and Reya here is your mother, Tana."

Agnes rushes towards her parents, and all three began to cry.

By this time, Roti was already blind in one eye and Tana's eyes were equally dim from hours of being kept in a dark room.

"Why Aunt Kiki, Why?" Agnes asks, sobbing.

"I'm sorry," Kiki replies, equally sobbing, "but we did it for you; no one would have married you, if they knew the circumstances of your birth."

* * *

Roti Disa had loved Tana Kembe since she was a young girl and the two had often talked about getting married and having twelve children. But Roti soon learnt that Yaya Pedro, the village terror, was about to ask for Tana's hand in marriage, and that same day, took his parents to Tana's, to register his intention.

Unable to afford Tana's bride price, however and the Disas were soon sent on their way. Roti wept like a baby; the thought of his beloved Tana being married to Yaya Pedro was more than he could bear. Yaya already had six wives, and all looked very miserable. Surely, Tana deserved better.

One morning, however, as Tana walked to the stream, with her friends, she was abducted on Roti's instructions, and immediately whisked away to some unknown destination. But the villagers soon found out and vowed to burn Roti's house if the young girl wasn't returned to her family.

Tana was brought back home, but ran back to Roti, as she was now with child.

* * *

Mama and Papa Kembe were very furious, and demanded that their daughter's bride price be paid, without any delay. But Roti was unable to meet the family's requirements, and was immediately sent to work on the Kembe family farm until he could afford to pay Tana's bride price. With that, Roti and Tana were exiled to the outskirts of the village.

* * *

A few months later, a heavily pregnant Tana joined Roti on the farm, only to go into labour. Agnes was born and immediately handed over to Kiki Gimera, and with it, a well-rehearsed story of how her parents had both lost their lives in a boating accident.

Everyone's Child

The Disas asked to raise their grand-daughter on behalf of their son but were refused. Roti hadn't paid Tana's bride price, they were told, so Agnes would remain a "Kembe".

Tana wept for days; she hadn't been allowed to hold her daughter, let alone breast feed her, and then, of course, her milk began to dry up. At this point, Tana Kembe became inconsolable, crying day and night as she longed for her baby girl.

* * *

A few years later, Papa and Mama Kembe passed away, leaving Kiki Gimera in charge of her younger sister, Tana, who was soon put to work the Gimera household, with Roti, but not before their identities had been changed. Tana was to be known as Reya, never to be seen in public and always with a black head-scarf, tied firmly around her distinctive forehead, while Roti was to become Dalu and instructed to grow a beard, and with it of course, strict instructions for both parents to stay away from their daughter and from the outside world.

And so Roti and Tana watched Agnes grow, unable to love or talk to her like other parents did.

* * *

But now in their old age, and still not married, Roti having been unable to afford Tana's bride price despite having worked for it all his life, Roti and Tana had asked for one last favour-to see their daughter one more time.

* * *

Agnes held onto her parents and sobbed until she hadn't any strength left, and at that moment, began remembering the times, when as a little girl, she had seen Tana watch her play in the yard, sometimes with tears in her(Tana's) eyes.

Roti, on the other hand, had often made his daughter little gifts from scraps around the house, telling her how special she was, but of course, Agnes didn't understand.

* * *

The next day, Agnes was on her way back to Muna, but with a promise to return the following week. However, the villagers soon found out what the Gimeras had been up to and immediately besieged their house.

And of course, Kiki had always maintained that her very "dedicated" cook and gardener were very distant relatives who had come to stay.

The Gimeras were instantly stripped of their titles and asked to relinquish all they'd been given by the village head.

Seeing however, that Agnes had been well taken care of, Lajo and Kiki were allowed to continue living in the village, albeit as ordinary people.

* * *

A few days later, and the elders of Lose were reviewing their bride pricing "policy", setting an upper limit on how much a man should be made to pay for his bride, a move that was welcomed by many from within the community. But for some, this change had come too late, particularly for those who like Roti had been unable to afford a wife in their youth, and had already resigned themselves to a life of singleness.

Everyone's Child

* * *

And Agnes did return the following week, and this time for her parents, Kamil having agreed that she could bring Roti and Tana over.

That same evening, the Gimeras formally handed Tana over to Roti as his bride, thirty-eight years after he abducted her on the way to the stream. Roti began to sob-how he longed for his family to be present, but of course, his parents were long gone and his three sisters were married and left the village. And then of course, Kiki and Lajo began asking for forgiveness, each blaming the other for the way things had turned out.

* * *

Agnes began to sob; her parents had been treated very badly indeed, but she was determined not to hold any grudges all the same- the Gimeras had given her every opportunity to succeed in life. She owed a lot to them. The only explanation, perhaps, was that Kiki and Lajo were victims of tradition, further compounded by their own greed.

Chapter Seventeen

Roti and Tana Disa spent the first few days of their freedom talking about anything and everything, for even though the two had both worked in the same household, they hadn't been allowed to talk freely with each other. Returning home one afternoon, Agnes soon noticed a change in her parents' appearance- Tana had ditched her trade mark black head scarf and had her grey hair neatly tied at the back of her head, while Roti was clean shaven.

"You both look so different," Agnes squeals, admiring her parents from every angle, only to then realize that she'd inherited her mother's distinctive forehead and her father's dimples, both of which had been hidden behind years of disguise.

* * *

But while Roti and Tana were making progress outwardly, both were still hurting, considerably, deep within.

And so began the process of healing, with Agnes encouraging her parents to let go of their hurt—she'd been there herself and knew how soul-destroying it could be.

Everyone's Child

* * *

Several months later, after hours of prayers and intense therapy, paid for by Kamil, Roti and Tana finally let go of their hurts and on the same day, accepted the Lord Jesus Christ into their lives.

Agnes couldn't be happier. Roti was still blind in one eye and walked with a limp, and Tana's eyes were still dim, but having her parents in the kingdom was more than she could have asked for.

* * *

And then came the news, Fay Gimera was getting married. Agnes was over the moon, and of course, she was to be a bridesmaid.

"At last," Tana muses, remembering how several prospective suitors had been turned away by the Gimeras for failing to meet their "requirements". One young man in particular had stood in the rain crying after he had been asked not to return, with or without his parents. He was John Batu and he loved Fay, dearly.

Kamil and Agnes decided to attend Fay's wedding together, leaving Joy with Roti and Tana, who were more than happy to have their grandson to themselves.

* * *

"And this is John," Fay says, excitedly, introducing her fiancé to the Bensons on their arrival. The young man could hardly contain his joy, either, smiling broadly as he shakes hands with Kamil. He was the same John, who had been asked not to return, with or without his parents, but thanks to a change in law, he was finally able to secure Fay's hand in marriage.

Determined to keep their presence in Lose a secret, however, Agnes and Kamil decided to stay with a friend of Fay's until the big day.

Chapter Eighteen

It's the morning of Fay's traditional wedding. John Batu's family have been seated for over an hour, waiting patiently or rather impatiently for their son's bride to show up, as was the custom. And then, a few minutes before noon, the bridesmaids began dancing in one after the other, their colourful attires lighting up the room. The drummers played their hearts out, beating on the leather drums with all their might as the girls wriggled their waists to the sound of the music.

And then Agnes danced in and suddenly all went quiet-she hadn't been expected to attend, not after the way her parents had been treated, even though she was to be a bridesmaid.

Kiki nearly fell off her chair and immediately held on to an equally shocked Lajo and throughout the afternoon kept looking up to see if her niece had come to disrupt the occasion.

* * *

But it soon became apparent that Agnes Benson had come in peace, as she stood up with other guests to give the Gimeras a gift, much to everyone's surprise. And with it, a letter, jointly thumbed by Roti and Tana, that all had been forgiven. This was more than the Gimeras had expected and right there in front of their guests, began to sob, thanking Agnes for being so forgiving.

* * *

The following morning, armed with numerous gifts for Roti and Tana, whose plights had prompted a change in the bride pricing "policy" in Lose, Agnes left for Muna with Kamil firmly by her side.

Chapter Nineteen

A few days after returning from Lose, Agnes Benson became seriously unwell. Totally convinced that their daughter had been poisoned at Fay's wedding, Roti and Tana began to cry, asking the Lord to keep Agnes alive for their sakes. But a quick visit to the hospital soon solves the mystery: Agnes was pregnant.

The Bensons were amazed, so were the doctors. No one could tell, how without a womb this could have happened. With that, Agnes Benson became a Case Study at the hospital, with her pregnancy being classed as a miracle, and the very first of its kind.

* * *

Nine months later, Benjamin was born, amidst cheering and clapping, and he was perfect in every way. Kamil hugs his wife and briefly offers a prayer of thanksgiving to the Lord. "We did it," he whispers into Agnes's left ear excitedly.

"We?" Agnes asks, weakly, smiling.

"I mean, you," Kamil replies, awkwardly, giving his wife a pat on the back.

Agnes shakes her head. "If only roles could have been reversed," she tells herself, as her husband began strolling around the delivery suite, hands in pocket.

* * *

Just then, the nurse hands Agnes a rather hungry Benjamin who latches on almost immediately.

"God has been so good to us," Kamil tells his wife, planting a kiss on her forehead.

"He sure has," Agnes replies, smiling.

A couple of days later, Benjamin was allowed home to a very excited Joy, who spent the afternoon ensuring that his baby brother was okay, much to everyone's delight.

* * *

And from then on, it was no stopping the Bensons until they'd decided they'd had enough, but not before Agnes had churned out three boys and two girls of her own, all within the space of eight years, and yes, without a womb.

For with God, nothing shall be impossible!

The End

www.ingramcontent.com/pod-product-compliance
Lightning Source LLC
Chambersburg PA
CBHW020319150626
46552CB00022B/2980